This book belongs to:

EMily

For Alasdair

First published 2017 by Walker Books Ltd

87 Vauxhall Walk, London SE11 5HJ

This edition published 2018

2 4 6 8 10 9 7 5 3 1

© 2017 Yasmeen Ismail

The right of Yasmeen Ismail to be identified as author/illustrator

of this work has been asserted by her in accordance with the

Copyright, Designs and Patents Act 1988

This book has been typeset in Bentham

Printed in China

British Library Cataloguing in Publication Data: a catalogue record

for this book is available from the British Library

ISBN 9781-4063-7887-0

www.walker.co.uk

WALKER BOOKS

AND SUBSIDIARIES

LONDON • BOSTON • SYDNEY • AUCKLAND

Yasmeen Ismail

Kiki and Bobo's

Sunny Day

Kiki and Bobo were having breakfast.

"It's so sunny this morning, Bobo," said Kiki.

"Do you know where I would like to go?"

"Where would you like to go, Kiki?" asked Bobo.

"To the seaside!" said Kiki.

Kiki packed her swimsuit and
put on her rubber ring.
"Where is your swimsuit, Bobo?" asked Kiki.

"I've lost it and I'm not sure I
will swim today," said Bobo.
"Maybe it's under your hat," said Kiki.

Bobo was very quiet on the bus to the beach. "I am so excited to swim in the sea," said Kiki. Bobo was not excited to swim in the sea. He wanted to go home.

"Let's have an ice cream," said Kiki.
"One for me, and one for you, Bobo."
Bobo did not feel like eating his ice cream
and he dropped it in the sand.

"Don't worry, Bobo," said Kiki.
"You can have some of mine."

"Shall we swim now, Bobo?" asked Kiki.
"No, Kiki," said Bobo, "we must put our sun cream on first."
"Good idea Bobo," said Kiki.

"Now shall we go swimming?" asked Kiki.
"No, Kiki, I would like to look for some shells first," said Bobo.

So they collected seashells all along the shore.

"Let's go swimming now!" said Kiki.
"No, Kiki," said Bobo, "I think we should
make a big sandcastle now."
"OK, Bobo," said Kiki, "but I want
to go swimming soon."

"Now it's time for swimming!" shouted Kiki.
"What's wrong, Bobo?"

"I'm scared of swimming in the sea," said Bobo, and he started to cry. Poor Bobo.

"Don't worry, Bobo," said Kiki. "You can use my rubber ring, and I'll stay with you the whole time. Would you like that?"

"Yes, Kiki," said Bobo, "I would like that very much." Kiki held Bobo's hand all the way into the sea. "I'm swimming, Kiki!" shouted Bobo.

That evening Kiki and Bobo
had a bath and then had tea.
"Thank you for helping me to swim, Kiki,"
said Bobo. "I'm not scared any more."

"You're welcome, Bobo," said Kiki.
"That's what friends are for!"

Also by Yasmeen Ismail:

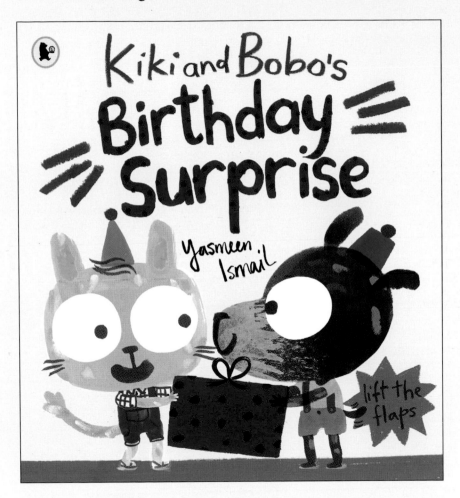

ISBN: 978-1-4063-8006-4